The Catnapping Cat

For Simon and Naomi – J.A

For my family – P.G

The Catnapping Cat
by Judy Allen and Philip Giordano

First published in 2006
by Hodder Children's Books
First published in paperback in 2007

Text copyright © Judy Allen 2006
Illustrations copyright © Philip Giordano 2006

Hodder Children's Books
338 Euston Road, London NW1 3BH

Hodder Children's Books Australia
Level 17/207 Kent Street,
Sydney NSW 2000

A catalogue record of this book is
available from the British Library.

10 9 8 7 6 5 4 3 2

ISBN: 9780340902707

Printed in China

Hodder Children's Books is a division of Hachette Children's Books.
An Hachette Livre UK Company.

The Catnapping Cat

Written by
Judy Allen

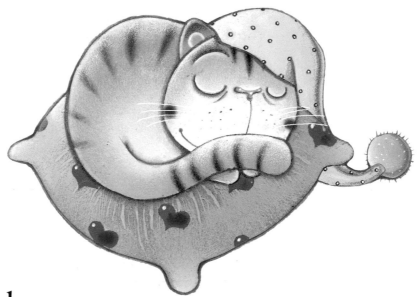

Illustrated by
Philip Giordano

Hodder
Children's
Books

A division of Hachette Children's Books

"I'VE CAST THOUSANDS OF SPELLS," said the witch to her cat.

"I've flown twice round the world, and my battery's flat.

It's been a long day. I need a good rest.

I wonder what kind of a place would be best."

"A bed is the best," said the witch's cat, Matt.

"It's cosy and warm and you can't beat that."

But the witch didn't listen and …

... she went on flying,

Till she saw a gorilla, who was peacefully lying,
In a nest of bent branches at the top of a tree,
And she said to her cat, "Now THAT would suit me."

She and her cat worked hard on their nest.

They struggled and strived; they both tried their best.

They followed each word of the gorilla's advice,

But it turned out all lumpy and not very nice.

"A bed is the best," said the witch's cat, Matt,
And he dreamt of a bed that was comfy and flat,
With cushions in velvet and pillows in satin,
All ready and waiting to welcome a cat in.

But the witch didn't listen and …

... she flew off once more,

Tilting the broomstick and making it soar,
Until high in the sky they met thousands of swifts,
Wings spread and eyes closed, sleeping in drifts.

"This is IT!" cried the witch, "Think of resting on air!"
("I'm thinking," her cat thought, "and I don't think I dare.")
The swifts tried to teach them – but they couldn't be taught.
It was too scary up there with just wind for support.

"A bed is the best," said the witch's cat, Matt,
And he dreamt (as his heart went rat-a-tat-tat),
Of a solid and safe and reliable mattress,
The perfect cure for the symptoms of cat stress.

But the witch didn't listen ...

… she'd spotted a mound,

With a hole in one side, and she knew what she'd found.
"It's the home of the badgers – they call it their sett.
It's the end of our search! It's the best haven yet!"

The badgers were wary, though they let them inside.
The burrows were stuffy and not very wide.
There wasn't much room and it was a strange feeling,
 Seeing worms and roots hanging out of the ceiling.

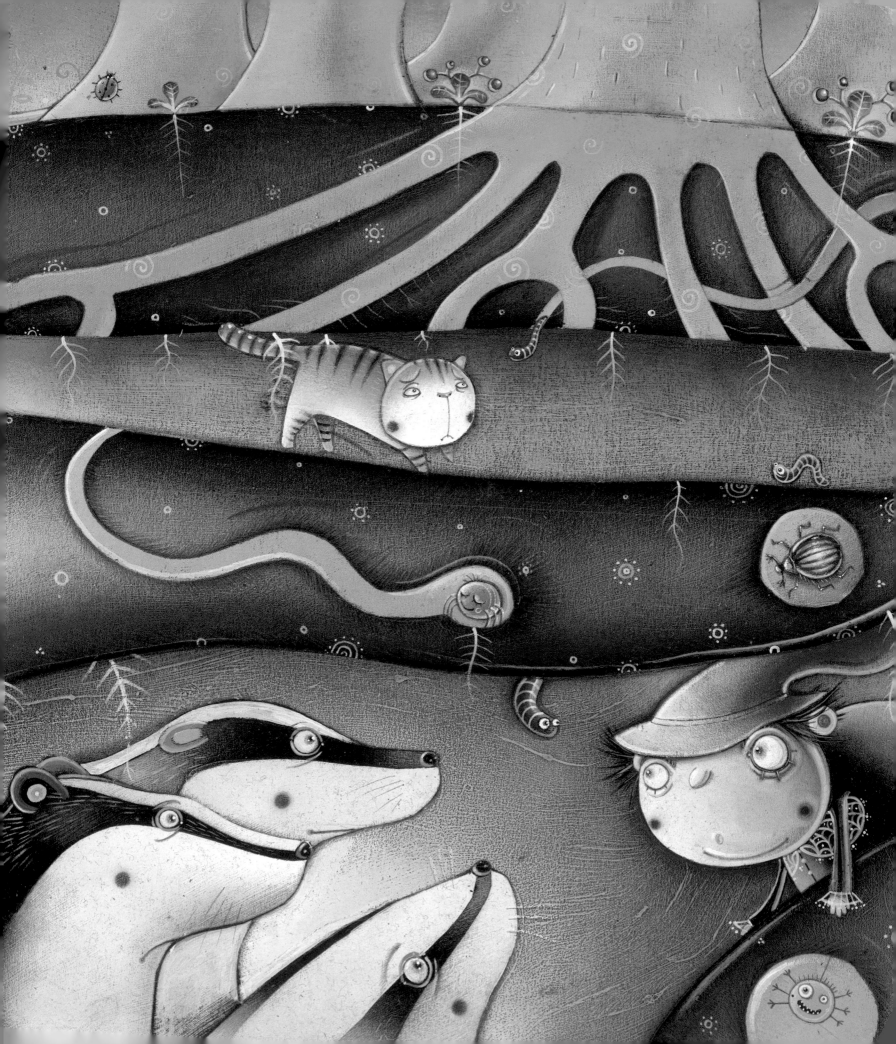

"I still say a bed's best," said the witch's cat, Matt.

And he dreamt of a cat-friendly place to be at.

Just a small bed would do – a crib, or a cot,

Somewhere worm-free and roomy – a nice airy spot.

But the witch didn't listen and …

… she flew off again,

Searching for somewhere more spacious, and then,
She noticed a cave, which was high, deep and wide,
With a flutter of bats, all flitting inside.

"Come hang from our roof!" called the tiny bat voices.
("This is not," thought the cat, "the best of our choices.")
The witch hung by her toes; the cat clung with each claw –
Then they both lost their grip and fell flat on the floor.

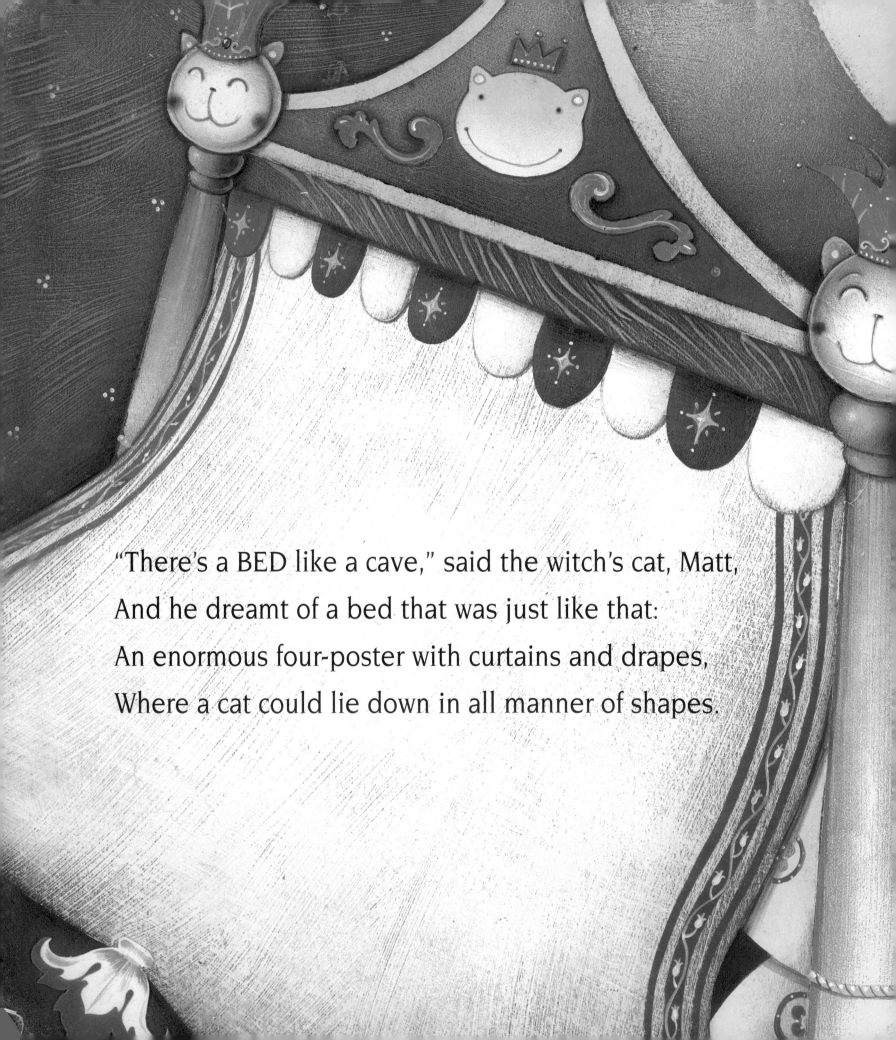

"There's a BED like a cave," said the witch's cat, Matt,
And he dreamt of a bed that was just like that:
An enormous four-poster with curtains and drapes,
Where a cat could lie down in all manner of shapes.

But the witch didn't listen ...

… she announced with a smile,

"I know a tree dweller who beds down in style.
You hate hanging and burrowing and floating and nesting,
But if we LIE on a branch you'll have no trouble resting."

She flew and she flew till she found what she sought,
A dozing tarantula who was a good sport.
The spider had woven herself a silk sheet.
She wove some for her guests – but they weren't very neat.

"Bed sheets are best," said the cobwebby Matt,
And he dreamt of sheets fit for an aristo-cat,
Of linen sheets, cotton sheets, sheets edged with lace,
And sheets made of silk that don't stick to the face.

But the witch didn't listen ...

... she flew to the shore,

Shouting, "I spy a sea otter! We'll search no more!
He rests on the water with his paws on his chest,
While the waves gently rock him. HIS way is best!"

The otter explained how to float on the swell.
They both tried their hardest – but it didn't go well.
"I think this," said cat Matt, "is your worst idea yet.
I feel silly and seasick and I hate being wet."

"A bed is the best," said the sad, soggy cat,
And he dreamt of this and he dreamt of that.
Of feathers or straw to be all dry and smug in,
Of luxurious rugs to be snug as a bug in.

But the witch didn't listen, she kept searching and snooping,
(Though her bones were aching and her eyelids were drooping),
Saying, "Not in a shell nor in any tight quarter,
And we'll drown if we join the fish underwater."

Then ...

… she turned to cat Matt – and guess what she said?
"*I* know what we need – we need our own bed.
It's warm, soft and cosy, it's clearly the best –
And it's so nice and big, let's invite all the rest!"

So in they all piled –

the gorilla
and spider,
the swifts
and sea otter,
all of the badgers
and every last bat ...

And who else?

Oh yes - the witch and cat Matt!